My Adopted Child, There's No One Like You

Dear Mama Bear and Papa Bear:

As you know, adoption is one of the most loving choices we have. In this story, young Panda now belongs to a loving family of bears. By book's end he feels very special, but first he has questions.

Some questions about adoption can be troubling for youngsters. We encourage you to talk to your child about adoption and let no subject be taboo. You may not have all the answers—or today may not be the appropriate time for your child to hear them—but talking openly as soon as possible will reap rewards down the road.

If you know details of your child's birth family, you will of course choose what to tell your child now, saving some details for when he or she is older. If you do not know details behind your little one's becoming available to you, avoid making up stories about it. Keep explanations simple and truthful. For example, it can be said about most adoptions that the adoptive parents wanted a child and a birth mother wanted a home for her child. Emphasize the love behind all the choices involved.

Families are born in the heart, Mama Bear explains to her Panda, and we hope their chat helps you share that wonderful concept with your child. And don't let the last page of this book go blank. Give your child a visual sense of belonging. While it's important for adopted children to feel good about adoption, it's just as important for them to feel like a solid member of the family. Be creative! You could even use your pet's picture in the frames. If some frames need to be added, that would be a fun art project. Each family is different in its own wonderful way.

The world is full of happy, successful adopted people. We hope this book shows your child how special he or she is today and forever.

My Adopted Child, There's No One Like You

Dr. Kevin Leman
& Kevin Leman II

Illustrated by
Kevin Leman II

Revell
Grand Rapids, Michigan

Text © 2007 by Dr. Kevin Leman and Kevin Leman II
Illustrations © 2007 by Kevin Leman II

Published by Fleming H. Revell
a division of Baker Publishing Group
P.O. Box 6287, Grand Rapids, MI 49516-6287
www.revellbooks.com

Printed in the United States of America

Library of Congress Cataloging-in-Publication Data

Leman, Kevin
    My adopted child, there's no one like you / Kevin Leman & Kevin Leman II ; illustrated by Kevin Leman II.
        p. cm.
    Summary: When Panda has to make a family tree for school, his mother explains how he came to be adopted, and how very special that makes him.
    ISBN 10: 0-8007-1889-5 (cloth)
    ISBN 978-0-8007-1889-3 (cloth)
    [1. Adoption—Fiction. 2. Pandas—Fiction. 3. Bears—Fiction. 4. Mother and child—Fiction.] I. Leman, Kevin, II. II. Title. III. Title: My adopted child, there is no one like you.
PZ7.L537345Mx 2007
[E]—dc22

                                                     2007015225

This book is affectionately dedicated to
Kayla Lauren Tucker,
the sweetest and most talented eight-year-old I know.
Kayla, you are loved and appreciated by so many people—
especially your mommy and daddy.

It was the end of the day at Forest School. Mrs. Racoonaroni called for quiet in the classroom.

"Before we leave today, students, I have an exciting assignment for you to do at home," she said. "Who knows what a family tree is?"

Panda had no idea what the answer to that was, but his friend Sidney Squirrel spoke up. "It's the tree where we live! Our family tree!"

Everyone giggled, and Mrs. Racoonaroni smiled. "It's certainly true that your family lives in a beautiful oak tree, Sidney. But I'm talking about something different."

Mrs. Racoonaroni picked up her chalk and drew a picture of a big tree on the blackboard. "This tree shows who your family is—your mother's family and your father's family—by putting their names on the different branches. And all those branches come from the same tree trunk."

Mrs. Racoonaroni put down her chalk and dusted her paws. "A family tree shows how your family came to be and how you belong to your family."

Panda didn't know if he liked this assignment. He thought it might be hard to do, because his family was different than all the other families in the classroom.

8

Just then the bell rang. All Forest School's students jumped up and hurried out the door.

"Hey Panda," called Sidney. "Wanna climb trees?"

Panda was not in a playful mood. "I have to get home," he said. And with that, he trudged right past Sidney.

Panda walked a little slower than usual down the forest path. He wasn't looking for mushrooms or listening to the birds chatter. He was thinking about his unusual family tree.

Instead of bounding into the kitchen for his afternoon snack, Panda slid silently through the doorway. Mama Bear heard him, and it was the strangest sound. It was the sound of—quiet!

Mama knew something was different.

P anda," Mama Bear called. "Are you there?"

Panda paused and sighed. "Yes, Mama, I'm here." He walked into the kitchen.

Mama put her fresh eucalyptus and honey cookies (a secret family recipe) on the table. She kept an eye on her cub as she poured a big glass of milk. "What's wrong, honeybear?" she asked.

Panda didn't touch his cookies. He sighed again. "Mrs. Racoonaroni wants us to draw our family tree."

Mama nodded. That certainly didn't seem to be a bad thing. "Why do you say it like that?"

"Because I'm adopted," he blurted out. "That means our family is different."

13

O h yes," said Mama Bear. "Our family is different." She beamed. "Very different indeed!"

Mama Bear took Panda's face in her paws and turned it toward her. "Have you heard Papa and me talk about how happy we are that we got to adopt you?"

Panda nodded, even though his chin was in Mama's paws.

Mama smiled again. "Well, it's true."

Panda pulled away. "But aren't we . . . different?" he stammered. "I mean, I don't even look like you and Papa. I mean, I . . . I'm a panda."

"Yes, we do look different. Papa and I are brown bears, and you're a black and white panda. And do you know what? We think you're the handsomest guy in the forest."

Panda's shoulders drooped.

"Oh honeybear, this is a good thing," said Mama Bear.

We're not just a different family. We're a special family. That's because we're a family built on love and love alone. We wanted you! We chose you!"

Panda thought that over. It did sound pretty special. Then he remembered the family tree assignment. "But where do I come from?"

Mama looked at Panda for a long moment. Then she said, "Let Mama tell you a story."

"Is this the story about grandpa eating all of grandma's pie before her company came over?"

"No, honeybear. You've never heard this story before. But I think you'll like it."

Mama Bear pulled Panda onto her lap. He snuggled into Mama's soft brown fur.

Once upon a time," Mama began, "there was a young panda who lived in a different forest from ours. She was going to have a baby. Now usually that's a happy time. But this panda was all alone and so young that she wondered how she could take care of a baby all by herself.

"That young panda thought and thought. She was very bright, and before long she knew what to do. She decided to find a family for her baby. It was the most loving thing she could do."

Mama Bear smiled—Panda could hear it in her voice. "That's where Papa and I came in. We wanted a baby so much. We put the word out to see if there was anyone who wanted a loving family for her cub. We waited a long time, and finally that panda mom found us. Oh, what a wonderful surprise!"

Mama Bear squeezed Panda. "I'll never forget that day."

"What did she look like, Mama?"

"Well, she was a beautiful black and white panda. She had sparkly eyes and a pretty nose, and she looked a lot like you. Most importantly, she was so kind. We knew we were getting a very special baby panda."

Mama pulled back and looked down at her cub. "That's adoption, honeybear. It's the most loving thing someone can do."

Panda thought this over. "You mean, she found a home for me because she loved me?"

"Oh yes. And Papa and I are so blessed! We got a little panda who is kind and loving."

Panda sat up straight. This story was different than he thought it would be. Different in a good way.

Mama Bear and Panda sat together for a while. Then Panda thought of something else. "Mama, where did she come from?"

"I'll show you on a map," Mama said. "And I think it's time you read about pandas. I have a book about them for you." Mama's voice got excited. "You know what?"

"What?"

"You can put all this in your family tree. Think about how interesting and special your family is!"

"Yeah," Panda said thoughtfully. "It is interesting."

"And special," said Mama, poking him gently in the ribs.

"Special," Panda repeated. It was true. He nodded. "Different, but special."

Mama Bear stroked her cub's paw. "God makes families, you know, all kinds of them. And God knew that you, Papa, and I would make a wonderful family."

Panda thought about that. He looked around the cozy den. He could smell the freshly baked cookies. He could see pictures of the fishing trip he took with Papa and his cousins. Finally he nodded. "We're a good family, Mama. Everyone says so."

"Do they?" Mama Bear said, laughing, and Panda shook on her lap. She squeezed him tightly. "Let me tell you one more thing."

"What's that, Mama?"

"You are the cub of my heart, Panda," said Mama. "You were born right here," and she touched her furry chest with her paw. "Don't ever forget that Papa and I love you very much and always will. We'll always be a part of each other, and even after you grow up, you'll always live in my heart."

Panda understood. Adoption was a special thing indeed. It came straight from the heart. "I love you too, Mama."

He slid off Mama Bear's lap. "I'm going to get my crayons," he announced. "I need to draw my family tree!" He grinned. "My different, interesting, exciting, special family tree!"

The next day, Panda presented his drawing of his family tree in front of the entire class. He felt very proud. And he did something extra special. He brought in a plate of his mom's eucalyptus and honey cookies. "It's a secret family recipe," he told his classmates.

"Mmmm," said Mrs. Racoonaroni. "I've never had these two things together in one cookie—eucalyptus and honey. It's very different. And very good."

Just like my family, thought Panda with a secret grin. And with that, he helped himself to another cookie.

The family tree Panda and Mama Bear
made looked a lot like this one.
But they put pictures in the frames.

So what goes into *your* family tree?
See the biggest frame?
That's for your picture.

Remember, it's okay to leave
some frames empty or to add more of them,
because it's *your* special family tree.

And because there's no one like you!

you!

For every cub in the forest

Dr. Kevin Leman & Kevin Leman II
My Only Child, There's No One Like You

Dr. Kevin Leman & Kevin Leman II
My Middle Child, There's One Like You

Dr. Kevin Leman & Kevin Leman I
My Youngest, There's No One Like You

Dr. Kevin Leman & Kevin Leman II
My Firstborn, There's No One Like You

Revell
www.revellbooks.com
a division of Baker Publishing Group